DISCARD

Lincoln County Library
Kemmerer, WY

ISBN : 978-1-85103-437-6
Originally published as Piotr Ilyich Tchaikovski by Éditions Gallimard Jeunesse
© Éditions Gallimard Jeunesse 2007
English text © 2015 Moonlight Publishing Ltd
This edition first published in the United Kingdom by Moonlight Publishing Ltd.
36 Innovation Drive, Milton Park, Abingdon, Oxon OX14 4RT
Printed in China

# Pyotr Ilyich TCHAIKOVSKY

## FIRST DISCOVERY MUSIC

Written by Stéphane Ollivier
Illustrations by Charlotte Voake
Narrated by John Chancer

## A CAREFREE CHILDHOOD

It is on 25 April 1840, with spring on its way, that Pyotr Ilyich Tchaikovsky is born, in Votkinsk, deep in the heart of snowbound Russia. His father, the director of a large ironwork, is an impressive figure of a man, while his

### BON VOYAGE MONSIEUR DUMOLLET

Like many Russians at the time, Tchaikovsky is brought up speaking French in the home. Many of the songs and nursery rhymes he grows up with are French ones. The second extract you are going to hear echoes the tune of a popular French children's song, 'Bon Voyage Monsieur Dumollet'.

Tchaikovsky's mother

**1** THE NUTCRACKER, 'MARCH'.
THE NUTCRACKER, 'CHILDREN'S GALLOP AND DANCE OF THE PARENTS'

mother is a beautiful, romantic young woman, whom he adores. Pyotr grows up in the cheerful company of his four rowdy brothers and his sister, watched over by Fanny, their young French governess, in the safety and comfort of a loving home.

## A MECHANICAL ORGAN

Pyotr is attracted by music from an early age. In the elegant living room of the Tchaikovsky home, alongside the grand piano, stands a strange instrument, an orchestrion. This giant musical box fascinates the small boy. He spends

The family around 1848

**2** 18 PIECES, OP. 72, 'TENDRES REPROCHES'

hours listening to renderings of different fashionable Italian operas of the day recorded on its rolls. His love of music is so strong that the family arranges piano lessons for him. On a real piano.

## PIANO CHORDS

A piano has 88 keys in all, 52 white, and 36 black, giving a wide range of different notes and tones. Have you had a chance to play some notes on a piano, or tease out a tune by ear? Do you know how to position your fingers on several different keys at once to produce a chord?

Tchaikovsky's mechanical organ

## A SENSITIVE LITTLE BOY

Pyotr is talented musically. Soon he is playing his favourite tunes and improvising elegant variations to them on the keyboard. His passion for music is all-consuming. Fanny worries about his health. Her "little

**Fanny Dürbach**
**Tchaikovsky's governess**

3 EUGENE ONEGIN, 'POLONAISE'

glass boy" is sensitive and frail and caught up by the force of his emotions. One night she finds him weeping in his bed, "It's the music. It's going round and round in my head. I can't get it to go away."

## MUSIC AND DANCE

The third act of "Eugene Onegin" opens with a lively polonaise, which was in origin a stately dance for two people in 3/4 time. Follow the beat and try to imagine what the steps of the dance might be.

## IN ST PETERSBURG

Pyotr is only twelve years old when he is sent away to study law in the great city of St Petersburg. He works hard at his studies, but he misses his mother and family, and the music he loved to play…

**4** VIOLIN CONCERTO IN D MAJOR, OP. 35, 'CANZONETTA'.
SYMPHONY NO. 4 IN F MINOR, OP. 36. 'FINALE. ALLEGRO CON FUOCO'

One evening, he goes to the magnificent opera house to see a performance of Don Juan, the opera by Mozart. He is captivated. His passion for music is re-awakened and he resolves to become a musician.

### LIVE MUSIC

In Tchaikovsky's day there was no television, radio or CDs. All music was live, played by musicians directly in front of their audience. Have you ever been to a concert, or listened to the strange rustling an orchestra makes when it is tuning up? Did you hold your breath as everything went quiet before the first notes were played?

## TURNED IN ON HIMSELF

Pyotr's life changes completely when his mother, whom he adores, dies suddenly from cholera. He is 14 years old and is overcome with grief. Pyotr turns in on himself in

**5** SYMPHONY NO. 5 IN E MINOR, 2ND MOVEMENT, 'ANDANTE CANTABILE CON ALCUNA LICENZA'

his sorrow. His passion for music begins to wane. He devotes all his time to studying law, graduates as a civil servant in the Ministry of Justice in 1859, and begins work as a clerk.

## MUSIC AND FEELINGS

**Music is undoubtedly the art which allows you to express strong emotions most directly: joy, lightheartedness, or deepest despair. Listen to the pieces on the CD and see if you can work out which feelings Tchaikovsky was expressing when he wrote them.**

Tchaikovsky as a law student in 1859

## RETURNING TO MUSIC

**P**yotr is now a good-looking young man about town, going to concerts, theatre and elegant receptions after finishing work. But he realises that something is missing from his carefree life. These social activities give

**6** THE SLEEPING BEAUTY, ACT I, NO. 5, 'SCENE' (THE PALACE GARDEN)

him no lasting satisfaction. He decides to enrol at the music conservatory which has just opened in his city, the St Petersburg Conservatory. The time has come to take music seriously.

## SHARPS AND FLATS

**Do you know what a sharp or a flat is? Or a whole note, half note or quarter note? These are all terms you learn when you begin to read music. Try tapping a two-time beat with your left hand on your left knee and three-time beat with your right hand on your right knee at the same time. You are already starting to learn some music theory.**

## TEACHER AND COMPOSER

Soon Pyotr is determined to become a composer. He decides to devote his life entirely to music. He resigns from his civil service job in order to concentrate entirely on music. He finds a job at the Moscow Conservatory teaching composition. He is 26 years old. His first symphony is written. His real career as a musician begins now, and will only end when he dies suddenly in 1893 at the age of 53.

## BECOMING A CONDUCTOR

You can have fun pretending to be the conductor of an orchestra or choir with your friends. Choose a song and agree on a code. Lift your arm, and they sing louder. Move your hands more quickly, and they sing more quickly. Wave your hands in a circle, and they start again. Close your hands, and they stop.

**7** THE NUTCRACKER, ACT I, SCENE 2, NO. 8 'A FIR FOREST IN WINTER'

**Today**

**as in the past**

**Tchaikovsky's**

**music**

**is played**

**and loved.**

## BALLET
# SWAN LAKE

It is perhaps in the ballet music he wrote, in the music scores specially composed to accompany a ballet performance, that Tchaikovsky shows himself to be a real master. *Swan Lake*, which is based on a fairy story, is a musical delight. Tchaikovsky demonstrates a remarkable talent for orchestration, and also makes each character in the ballet distinct and very real. In this piece the white swan, represented in the orchestra by the oboe, is dancing to one of the most poignant melodies ever written by the composer.

Tchaikovsky transformed the way people regarded ballet. Previously it had been considered a lesser art form. "Swan Lake", together with "The Nutcracker", are two of the most frequently performed of all ballets.

There is a great tradition of ballet in Russia, and many of the most talented ballet dancers in the the world have been Russian. From Pelageya Karpakova (who first played the role of the White Swan, Odette, in the Bolshoi ballet in 1877), to Pavlova, Nijinsky and Nureyev, all have danced in "Swan Lake".

**8** SWAN LAKE, ACT II, NO. 10 (OVERTURE)

## CONCERTOS
# THE PIANO CONCERTO

In the course of his career Tchaikovsky only ever composed two concertos, works in which a solo instrument has a conversation with the rest of the orchestra. One was written for piano, the other for violin. Though relatively few, these two works are masterpieces, full of colour, feeling and furious rhythms. Listen to the cascade of notes in the piano concerto. They mark out a melody, which the string instruments in the orchestra then take up. In just a few musical phrases Tchaikovsky's lyricism breaks forth.

Tchaikovsky composed all his music and presented his operas and symphonies to his friends on the piano. At the age of 14, Tchaikovsky was taught by the famous piano-maker, Becker. We see here Piotr's piano in his house in Klin.

Nadezhda von Meck, a widow and great admirer of Tchaikovsky, provides him with a generous sum of money for many years, which enables him to live comfortably. Throughout this time, the two carry on a long and intimate correspondence, without ever actually meeting face to face.

**9** PIANO CONCERTO NO. 1 IN B-FLAT MINOR, 'ALLEGRO NON TROPPO E MOLTO MAESTOSO'

## OPERA
# EUGENE ONEGIN

Tchaikovsky composed many pieces for the human voice: more than a hundred songs and no less than eleven operas. An opera is like a form of musical theatre in which the actors sing rather than speak. Writing an opera demands highly specialised skills; the composer needs to have a sense of drama, real talent as a melody writer, and an ability to translate action and feeling into music, which the orchestra can play. The best of Tchaikovsky's operas, the *Queen of Diamonds* and *Eugene Onegin* are both adaptations of tales by the famous Russian author, Alexander Pushkin.

The famous author, Alexander Pushkin (1799-1837), provides the theme for Tchaikovsky's opera: Onegin, an idle, worldly, and selfish young man rejects Tatyana's love for him, and turns his attentions to his friend Lenski's fiancée. Lenski summons him to a duel, and is killed. When Onegin meets Tatyana again some years later, he falls in love with her... but it is too late.

Russian popular music is essentially vocal, and opera is the art form that attracted most Russian composers. Tchaikovsky was so captivated by the opera singer Desirée Artôt that he nearly married her.

**10** EUGENE ONEGIN, ACT I, SCENE 2, NO. 9, 'LETTER SCENE' (TATYANA, ONEGIN)

## THE SYMPHONIES
# THE PATHÉTIQUE

Tchaikovsky knew better than anybody how to express in music the extraordinary mixture of gaiety (lightheartedness) and profound sadness which make up the Russian character. The six symphonies he wrote allow each instrument in the orchestra its voice and are rather like a series of confessions filled with feelings and emotion, which he pours forth in sound. The most intense of these is his sixth symphony, written shortly before his own death, in which he expresses the eternal struggle between life and death.

An orchestra is a group of different instruments, consisting of strings, brass, woodwind, and percussion. Large orchestras are known as symphony or philharmonic orchestras. Smaller orchestras are known as chamber orchestras. Tchaikovsky's orchestral pieces give pride of place to trumpets and trombones.

A symphony is an instrumental piece. Unlike an opera it often has no precise theme or "programme", although Tchaikovsky claimed to have a theme in mind when he wrote the "Pathétique", but would not reveal what it was. It remains a mystery.

▶ 11  SYMPHONY NO. 6 IN B MINOR, "PATHÉTIQUE", FINALE, 'ADAGIO LAMENTOSO'

## MOONLIGHT PUBLISHING

**Translator**
Penelope Stanley-Baker

**English narration recording**
Matinée Sound & Vision Ltd

---

## GALLIMARD JEUNESSE

**Director
Gallimard Jeunesse Musique :**
Paule du Bouchet

**Recording and mixing :**
Studios Davout

## LIST OF ILLUSTRATIONS

**6t** Map of Europe created by Paul Coulbois, 2007, © Paul Coulbois / Gallimard Jeunesse. **6bl** The mother of Pyotr Ilyich Tchaikovsky, Alexandra Andreyevna Tchaikovsky, © Roger-Viollet. **6br** Tchaikovsky's home in Votkinsk, Tchaikovsky Museum in Votkinsk / Siny Most. **8** The Tchaikovsky family in 1848 in Votkinsk (from left to right, seated: Alexandra Andreyevna Tchaikovsky, Alexandra, Hippolyta, Ilya Petrovitch Tchaikovsky ; standing: Pyotr, Zinaïde, the half sister of Pyotr, and Nicolas), © Tchaikovsky Museum in Votkinsk / Siny Most.
**9** The Tchaikovsky's mechanical organ © Tchaikovsky Museum in Votkinsk / Siny Most. **10** Fanny Durbah, Tchaikovsky's French governess, © Tchaikovsky Museum in Votkinsk / Siny Most. **11** A. Pakhromenko, *Tchaikovsky as a child*, © Tchaikovsky Museum in Votkinsk / Siny Most. **13h** St Petersburg, Nevsky Prospect, coloured lithograph , XIX siècle. Paris. Bibliothèque nationale de France, © Photo RMN / Bulloz. **13b** Alexei Filipovitch Tchernicheff (1824-1863), *The Organ Grinder*, St Petersburg 1852, oil on canvas. Moscow, Tretyakov Gallery, © akg-images. **15l** Tchaikovsky as a law student in 1859, © Tchaikovsky Museum in Votkinsk / Siny Most. **15d** Tchaikovsky's law class in 1859 in St Petersburg, © Tchaikovsky Museum in Votkinsk / Siny Most. **16** Franz Skarbina (1849-1910), *Ball at the Opera House*, around 1900, oil on canvas. Wuppertal, Von der Heydt Mueum, © akg-images. **19** Portrait of Pyotr Tchaikovsky around 1893 by Nikolai Dmitrievich Kuznetsov (1850-1930), oil on canvas, © The Bridgeman Art Library / Tretyakov Gallery, Moscow. **20t** *Swan Lake*, ballet, choreography by Rudolf Nureyev. National Opera of Paris Ballet. with Agnès Letestu. December 2005. © Ramon Senera / Agence Bernand. **20m** *The Nutcracker Suite*, ballet. choreography by Marius Petipa, Mihail Chemiakin et Kiril Simonov. Châtelet Theatre, Paris October 2002, © Colette Masson / Roger-Viollet. **20b** The ballerina Karpakova, who first played the role of Odette in *Swan Lake*, at the Bolshoi Theatre in Moscow in 1877, © Rue des Archives / Lebrecht. **21** Edgar Degas (1834-1917), *A Group of dancers*, oil on canvas, around 1884-85. The Louvre, Paris, D.A.G. , © Photo RMN / Patrice Schmidt. **22t** *Pyotr Ilyich Tchaikovsky*, illustration, around 1893, © Rue des Archives / Lebrecht. **22m** Tchaikovsky's grand piano in Klin, photo, 1993, © akg-images / Vsevolod M. Arsenyev. **22b** Nadzehda von Meck, patron and friend of Tchaikovsky (1831-1894), © Rue des Archives / Lebrecht. **23** Andrei Petrovich Ryabushkin (1861-1904), *A Lad has wormed his way into the Girls' Round*, oil on canvas Tretyakov Gallery, Moscow. © Bridgeman Giraudon. **24t** Alexander Pushkin, Russian poet, playwright and author (1799-1837). Portrait by Orest A. Kiprenski (1782-1836). Oil on canvas. Tretyakov Gallery, Moscow © akg-images Paris. **24m** Desirée Artôt, French soprano (1835-1907). photograph around 1872, by Hanns Hanfstaengl, Berlin, © akg-images Paris. **24b** *Eugene Onegin* by The English National Opera in the Coliseum Theatre, London, June 2005, © Rue des Archives/Lebrecht. **26t** Symphony orchestra, © Getty Images. **26m** A conductor's hands, © Getty Images. **26b** A manuscript page from the score of the opera *Eugene Onegin* written in Moscow in 1879. Glinka Museum of Musical Culture, Moscow, © akg-images. **27** Egon Schiele (1890-1918), Austrian painter and set designer, *Self portrait*. Water colourand crayon, 1912. Private collection. © akg-images, Paris.

KEY:   **t** = top   **m** = middle   **b** = bottom   **r** = right   **l** = left

## CD

**1. A carefree childhood**
*The Nutcracker*, Act I, Scene I, No. 2,
'March'
Royal Concertgebouw Orchestra
Conductor Antal Dorati
From CD "The Nutcracker/
The Sleeping Beauty" (Philips Duo)
Recording: Amsterdam 1975.
℗ 1994 Philips Classic Production

*The Nutcracker*, Act I, Scene I, No. 3,
'Children's Gallop and Dance of the
Parents'

Royal Concertgebouw Orchestra
Conductor Antal Dorati
From CD "The Nutcracker/
The Sleeping Beauty" (Philips Duo)
Recording: Amsterdam 1975.
℗ 1994 Philips Classic Production

**2. Mechanical piano**
*18 pieces Op. 72*,
'Tendres reproches' in C-sharp minor
Mickhail Pletnev, piano
From CD "Tchaikovsky: 18 Piano
Pieces Op. 72 / Mickhail Pletnev"
(Deutsche Grammophon)
Recording: Zurich. 2004.
℗ 2005 Deutsch Grammophon GmbH.
Hamburg

**3. A sensitive little boy**
*Eugene Onegin*, Act III, Scene 1, No.
19, 'La Polonaise'
Berlin Philharmonic
From CD boxed set "Karajan conducts
Tchaikovsky" (Deutsche Grammophon)
Recording: Berlin, 1970.
℗ 1972. Polydor International GmbH.
Hambourg

**4. In St Petersburg**
*Violin Concerto in D major*, Op. 35,
2nd Movement, 'Canzonetta'. Andante
Berlin Philharmonic
Conductor Herbert von Karajan
Christian Ferras, violin
From CD boxed set "Karajan conducts
Tchaikovsky" Recording: Berlin, 1965.
℗ 1966. Polydor International GmbH.
Hamburg

*Symphony No. 4 in F minor*, Op 36,
'Finale. Allegro con fuoco'
Berlin Philharmonic
Conductor Herbert von Karajan
From CD boxed set "Karajan conducts
Tchaikovsky" (Deutsche Grammophon)
Recording: Berlin. 1966.
℗ 1967. Polydor International GmbH.
Hamburg

**5. Turned in on himself**
*Symphony No. 5 in E minor*, Op. 64,
2nd Movement, 'Andante cantabile, con
alguna licenza'
Berlin Philharmonic
Conductor Herbert von Karajan
From CD boxed set "Karajan conducts
Tchaikovski" (Deutsche Grammophon)
Recording: Berlin, 1965.
℗ 1966. Polydor International GmbH.
Hamburg

**6. Returning to music**
*The Sleeping Beauty*, Op. 66,
Act 1, No. 5, 'Scene' (The Palace Garden)
London Symphony Orchestra
Conductor Anatole Fistoulari
From CD "The Nutcracker/
The Sleeping Beauty" (Philips Duo)
Recording: London. 1962.
℗ 1994 Philips Classic Production

**7. Teacher and composer**
*The Nutcracker*, Act I, Scene II, No. 8
'A Fir Forest in Winter'
Royal Concertgebouw Orchestra
Conductor Antal Dorati
Extract from CD "The Nutcracker/
The Sleeping Beauty" (Philips Duo)
Recording: Amsterdam 1975.
℗ 1994 Philips Classic Production

**8. Ballet**
*Swan Lake*, Op. 20, Act II, No. 10
(overture). Moderato
Boston Symphony Orchestra
Conductor Seiji Ozawa
From the CD "Tchaikovsky: Swan
Lake" (Deutsche Grammophon).
℗ 1979. Polydor International GmbH.
Hamburg

**9. Concertos**
*Piano Concerto No. 1 in B-flat minor*,
Op. 23, 1st Movement, 'Allegro non
troppo e molto maestoso'
Berlin Philharmonic
Conductor Herbert von Karajan
From the CD boxed set "Karajan
conducts Tchaikovsky" (Deutsche
Grammophon)
Recording: Vienna, 1962.
℗ 1972. Polydor International GmbH.
Hamburg

**10. Opera**
*Eugene Onegin*, Act I, Scene 2, No. 9
'Letter Scene' (Tatyana, Onegin)
Orchestre de Paris
Conductor Semyon Bychkov
St Petersburg Chamber Choir
Nuccia Focile, Tatyana
Olga Borodina, Olga
From the CD "Tchaikovsky:
Eugene Onegin" (Philips)
Recording: 1992
℗ 1993 Universal Music International BV

**11. Symphonies**
*Symphony No. 6 in B minor*, Op. 74
"Pathétique", 4th Movement, 'Adagio
lamentoso'
Berlin Philharmonic
Conductor Herbert von Karajan
From the CD boxed set "Karajan
conducts Tchaikovsky" (Deutsche
Grammophon)
Recording: Vienna. 1964.
℗ 1964. Polydor International GmbH.
Hamburg

**FIRST DISCOVERY MUSIC**

LOUIS ARMSTRONG
JOHANN SEBASTIAN BACH
LUDWIG VAN BEETHOVEN
HECTOR BERLIOZ
FRYDERYK CHOPIN
CLAUDE DEBUSSY
GEORGE FRIDERIC HANDEL
WOLFGANG AMADEUS MOZART
HENRY PURCELL
FRANZ SCHUBERT
PYOTR ILYICH TCHAIKOVSKY
ANTONIO VIVALDI

Lincoln County Library
Kemmerer WY